The Princess and the Moon

Written by
DAISAKU IKEDA

Illustrated by
BRIAN WILDSMITH

English version by
GERALDINE McCAUGHREAN

Oxford University Press

OXFORD TORONTO MELBOURNE

Like a bright, cheerful face, the silver Moon shines down at night
on the homes of children everywhere: on happy and sad children,
loving and unkind, sensible and foolish.

Did you ever think it might be looking down at you?
Sophie never dreamt of such a thing.

But not long ago, Sophie looked out of her window to see the Great
Moon Rabbit leaping and loping down a beam of moonlight, its eyes
afire and its long ears heavy with stardust.

Like the Moon it waxed and waned, sometimes huge, sometimes small, and its fur glistened with flecks of light.

Both fierce and trembling, both gentle and frightening, it landed amid the flowers of the night garden; its paws sank softly into the earth, and its fur rippled in an astral wind.

'The Moon has been watching you, Sophie, and is not pleased by
what he has seen. Take hold of my paw. You are to come with me.'

Before she could protest, Sophie found herself soaring up the
towering shaft of moonlight towards the battered face of Old Moon.
'What have I done? Is it because I'm so bad-tempered?

Is it because I'm so ugly – so useless at school? Is it because nobody
likes me? Is the Moon angry with me?'
 But the Moon Rabbit would not answer.

In an age and in an instant, Sophie found herself flying towards an archway of starry light – entrance to the Country of the Moon. From inside came the sound of laughter and games – of children playing happily together. And when the gates opened, the sight that met her eyes was at once faintly familiar and wonderfully strange.

Everywhere children were playing or
dancing, singing or talking. Each wore a
crown and a cape of golden tissue. She
called out to them but they did not
answer. A king and queen passed by,
bending their heads to listen to their
daughter – a princess of great beauty and
grace. And yet when the princess looked
up, her face was one Sophie had seen so
often as she looked in the mirror.

'Yes, Sophie,' said the Great Moon Rabbit. 'The king and queen are your mother and father. The princess is you. The other children are all your school-friends.'

'So that's why they won't speak to me,' said Sophie sadly.

'They don't speak because they aren't here,' said the Rabbit. 'These are just the Shinings of children on Earth – each boy and girl as he and she really is.'

'As they really are? Oh, nonsense! I know that girl – it's Pat,' said Sophie, pointing rudely. 'She never joins in at school! Always sour-faced, always quarrelling. Nobody likes her.'

'But here you see her as she really is, underneath her shyness and loneliness: as she would be if she were treated like a princess. Underneath, everyone deserves that, you know.'

'See over there where the Sophie-on-the-Moon sits down to dinner with the king and queen. Always smiling. Always cheerful. Always helpful. Always patient. Always looking forward to the good things in store.'

'Then she's not one bit like me,' said Sophie enviously.

'What do you mean?' asked the Rabbit. 'She is just the Shining of Sophie-on-the-Earth.'

'But she's so pretty in that crown and that golden cape.'

'Oh, it's not the clothes,' said the Great Rabbit. 'It's just that she's wearing a smile and an open heart.'

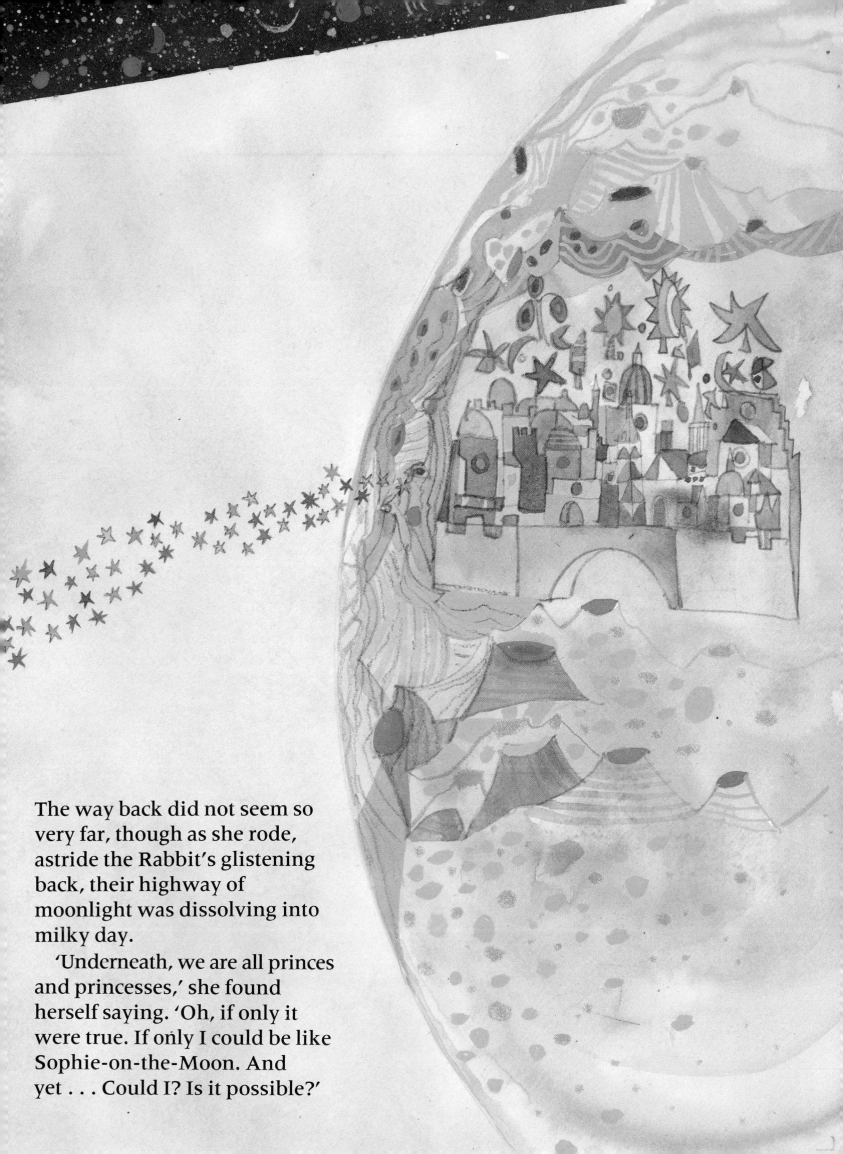

The way back did not seem so very far, though as she rode, astride the Rabbit's glistening back, their highway of moonlight was dissolving into milky day.

'Underneath, we are all princes and princesses,' she found herself saying. 'Oh, if only it were true. If only I could be like Sophie-on-the-Moon. And yet . . . Could I? Is it possible?'

'Don't go!' she called to the figure standing moonlit in the window. 'You could help me to be like a Princess all the time!'

'You don't need any help,' said the Great Rabbit. 'You have learned a lot tonight.'

'But it will be so much harder when no one wears a crown! So easy to be ordinary and small and mean.'

'No crown?' said the Rabbit. 'But all you Children-on-the-Earth have crowns, my dear. It's just that they don't show in the sunlight.'

Knowing that, of course, it was easy for Sophie-on-the-Earth – the next day and every day – to smile, to be kind, to be gracious. For she had learned to look as the Moon looks, with royal, bright, and caring eyes. And to see the things that matter.

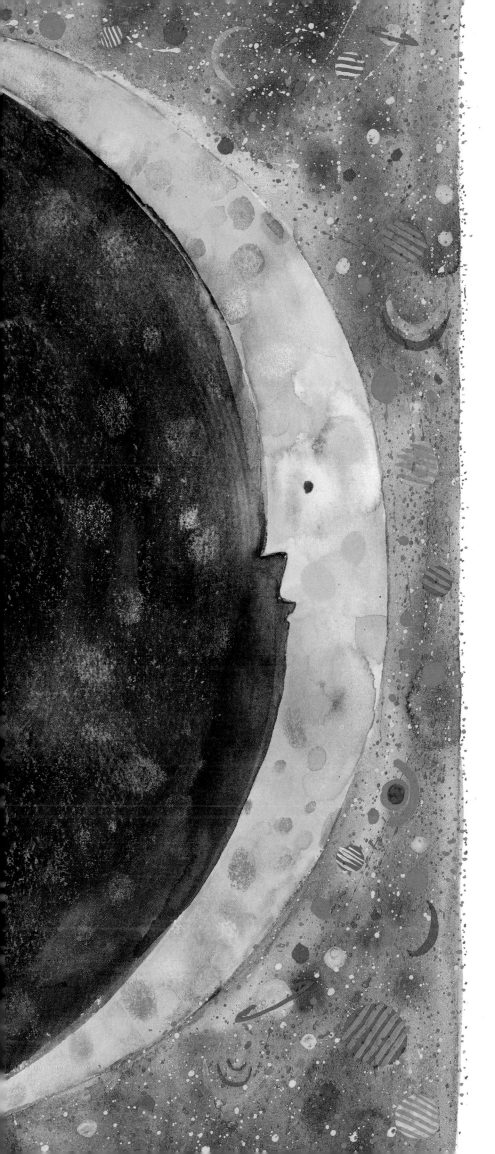

'You were worried about Sophie,' said the Great Rabbit to the Moon. 'Always bad-tempered, never smiling, out-of-step at school.'

'Was I?' said the forgetful Moon vaguely. 'Surely not. Why, look now! When she sings all the planets stop to listen, and when she smiles the stars turn somersaults. No, no, you're mistaken, Rabbit. I must have meant some other little girl.'

The Great Rabbit said nothing, but wiped a little stardust off an ear with one paw and beamed as brightly as the Moon itself.

Oxford University Press, Walton Street, Oxford OX2 6DP

Oxford is a trade mark of Oxford University Press

Text © Daisaku Ikeda 1991
Illustrations © Brian Wildsmith 1991
English Version © Geraldine McCaughrean 1991
First translated from the Japanese by Burton Watson

A CIP catalogue record for this book is available from the British Library

ISBN 0 19 271680 8

Typeset by Pentacor PLC
Printed in Hong Kong